D0827659

Agatha
Girl of Mystery

GROSSET & DUNLAP
Published by the Penguin Group
Penguin Group (USA) LLC, 375 Hudson Street, New York, New York 10014, USA

USA | Canada | UK | Ireland | Australia | New Zealand | India | South Africa | China

penguin.com
A Penguin Random House Company

If you purchased this book without a cover, you should be aware that this book is stolen property. It was reported as "unsold and destroyed" to the publisher, and neither the author nor the publisher has received any payment for this "stripped book."

Penguin supports copyright. Copyright fuels creativity, encourages diverse voices, promotes free speech, and creates a vibrant culture. Thank you for buying an authorized edition of this book and for complying with copyright laws by not reproducing, scanning, or distributing any part of it in any form without permission. You are supporting writers and allowing Penguin to continue to publish books for every reader.

Original Title: Agatha Mistery: La Corona del Doge
Text by Sir Steve Stevenson
Original cover and illustrations by Stefano Turconi

English language edition copyright © 2014 Penguin Group (USA) LLC. Original edition published by Istituto Geografico De Agostini S.p.A., Italy, 2011 © 2011 Atlantyca Dreamfarm s.r.l., Italy

International Rights © Atlantyca S.p.A.—via Leopardi 8, 20123 Milano, Italia
foreignrights@atlantyca.it—www.atlantyca.com

Published in 2014 by Grosset & Dunlap, a division of Penguin Young Readers Group, 345 Hudson Street, New York, New York 10014. GROSSET & DUNLAP is a trademark of Penguin Group (USA) LLC. Printed in the USA.

Library of Congress Cataloging-in-Publication Data is available.

10 9 8 7 6 5 4 3 2 1

ISBN 978-0-448-46225-7

Agatha

Girl of Mystery

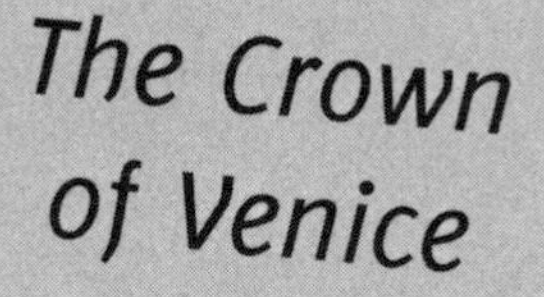

The Crown of Venice

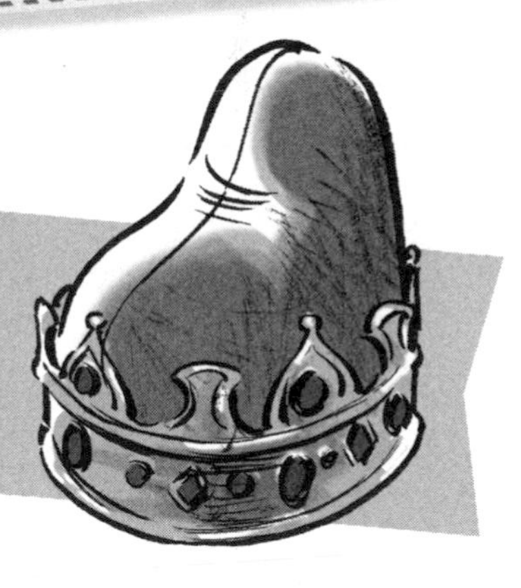

by Sir Steve Stevenson
illustrated by Stefano Turconi

translated by Siobhan Tracey
adapted by Maya Gold

Grosset & Dunlap
An Imprint of Penguin Group (USA) LLC

I would like to acknowledge the tireless assistance of Gianfrance Calvitti, a close friend and exceptional mystery writer.

SEVENTH MISSION

Agents

Agatha
Twelve years old, an aspiring mystery writer; has a formidable memory

Dash
Agatha's cousin and student at the private school Eye International Detective Academy

Chandler
Butler and former boxer with impeccable British style

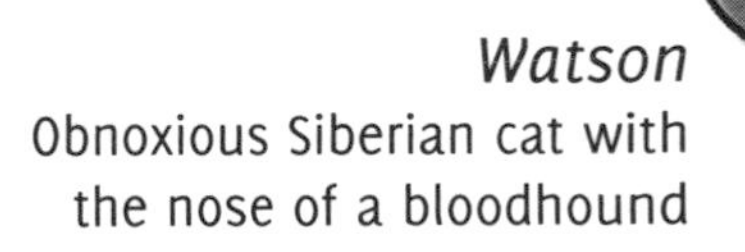

Watson
Obnoxious Siberian cat with the nose of a bloodhound

Marco
Gondolier who guides tourists through the canals of Venice; sings romantic ballads at the top of his lungs

DESTINATION

Venice, Italy

OBJECTIVE

Discover who stole a priceless golden crown that belonged to one of the Doges of the Most Serene Republic of Venice

PRELUDE

The Investigation Begins . . .

It was a Sunday morning in the middle of February, and a loud blare of trumpets rattled the window glass of the penthouse apartment above Baker Place. The stereo's surround sound was state of the art; it sounded as if General Custer himself had come back to life and was blowing a bugle into the ear of the tall teenage boy stretched out on the sofa.

Dashiell Mistery jolted awake, as quickly as if someone had thrown him under an ice-cold shower. His hair flopped over his forehead as he clapped his hands over his ears and jumped into action, dodging piles of clothes and stray electronic devices to slam down the volume control on his stereo. The trumpets cut off midnote.

Dash stood panting with relief, his eyes puffy from lack of sleep. It was eight in the morning. His brand-new alarm system had done the trick, but the fourteen-year-old student at Eye International Detective Academy couldn't remember why in the world he had set it to go off so early. He scratched his head as memories

of the previous night began to seep through the fog around his brain. "Oh no," he groaned in despair. "My Criminal Physiognomy class! I'd better get to work!"

In a flash, he was sprawled in his swivel chair, staring at his army of computers. Every one of the monitors was displaying *Alien Hunt*, an online video game in which a squad of action heroes patrols a space station, wiping out monsters from outer space.

He'd spent most of the week using the avatar Phil Destroy, a cyborg warrior armed to the teeth. In a week of marathon sessions, Dash had worked his way up to the national finals, taking on top-ranked players with names like Killderella and Exterminizer. Meanwhile, he'd completely neglected his Criminal Physiognomy homework, and now he was terrified that Professor FB32, who had a sixth sense for sniffing out slackers, would pick on him to answer questions in the class's next videoconference.

Would he make a fool of himself? In just a few minutes, his teacher's face would appear on the screen. He had to get ready immediately!

Feeling frantic, Dash logged off *Alien Hunt* and picked up the printouts and notes strewn all over his desk. He formed a mound of paper in front of him, picked up a yellow highlighter, and started to cram. Physiognomy was a difficult subject—it involved looking for clues about a person from their appearance, especially facial features.

"Okay, okay . . . 'What does it mean when the subject has a unibrow?'" Dash muttered to himself. He searched through his notes until he found a scrawl on the back of a candy wrapper. "Ah, here we go," he went on. "It's a clear sign of an inclination toward theft!"

He narrowed his eyes and continued to work his way down the review questions. "'Who came up with this theory?'" he read aloud.

Dash didn't need to dig through his notes for the answer to this question. "Simple!" he crowed. "Cesare Lombroso, the founder of criminal anthropology. Which was later debunked by two other professors . . . wait, what were their names again?" He rifled through his pile of paper.

"Where are my historical notes?" he cried in desperation. He remembered that Cesare Lombroso's nineteenth-century theories had been revised from top to bottom. But who had done it, and why?

"I don't have a clue," he groaned. "I really need to pay more attention and take better notes! Now what will I tell the professor?"

To make matters worse, the Eye International symbol suddenly flashed on the monitor screen of his main computer, followed by a message: *Connecting, please wait.*

Dash ran his hands through his hair. "I'm

sunk!" he repeated again and again.

But weirdly, the face that appeared on his screen was not his professor's, but that of the school secretary, a middle-aged woman with frown lines framing her mouth. "We're sorry to inform you that Agent FB32 is engaged in a mission and won't be able to teach today's class," she announced. "The Criminal Physiognomy class is postponed until next Sunday. Happy investigating, everyone!"

The smile on Dash's face spread from one ear to the other. What amazing luck! Now he had a whole week to revisit the topic and take better notes, and he decided to start right away. But his stomach was growling. It wouldn't hurt to have something for breakfast first, would it? He picked up the phone and ordered his favorite breakfast: a three-cheese pizza with double pepperoni, anchovies, and jalapeños. He'd nicknamed it "Zombie Pizza" because the smell alone could wake the dead.

He had just put down the phone when a *BLIP!* let him know that his friends were online for a game of *Alien Hunt.*

"I can't give in to temptation," Dash lectured himself. "I have to focus on my detective career."

But his resistance crumbled in seconds. *I've got a whole week,* he told himself. He swiveled to face his computer, put on his headset, and greeted Clarke and Mallory, whose avatars were waiting for him at the entrance to the first level. Phil Destroy entered the dark corridors of the spaceship, overcome with the thrill of the challenge.

"Blast that monster! Zap it!" Clarke's voice shouted through the headphones.

"Look out! They're coming out of the walls!" Mallory yelled at the top of her lungs.

"I'll have to bounce pretty soon, guys," Dash interrupted. "I'm getting a pizza delivered."

"Hey Dash, did you hear about all the

apartment thefts?" asked Clarke.

"No, what happened?"

"Scotland Yard says every one of the victims had a pizza delivered right before they noticed their stuff had gone missing," his friend explained.

"It happened to us," added Mallory. "They stole my mom's silver teapot."

Dash snickered. If the police had called him to investigate, he would have solved the case by now.

"They wouldn't have much luck with me," he declared between blasts of his turbo-charged ray gun. "I'm much too smart to fall for a scam like that!"

The ring of the doorbell distracted Dash from the game. He swung the door open and welcomed the pizza delivery man. His name was

Derek; he was a nice guy who always told Dash wild stories about his deliveries around the city. And he didn't have a unibrow, so he was clearly not a thief!

"That'll be sixteen," said Derek.

After digging around on the table, Dash managed to unearth his wallet and hand over a twenty. Derek walked off, thanking him for the generous tip.

But the morning still had surprises in store. As he scarfed down his first slice of hot Zombie Pizza, the aspiring detective noticed that the special titanium device hanging on its hook above the sofa was flashing.

"Dash! What are you doing? We're getting annihilated!" Clarke's protests rang over the headphones.

Dash ignored him and grabbed his titanium EyeNet, the high-tech device used by every student at his detective school. The message on the screen made him immediately lose his appetite.

INVESTIGATION IN VENICE! UTMOST URGENCY.
CONSULT THE ATTACHED FILES ASAP.

Dash abandoned his half-eaten pizza and took off like an intercontinental missile to his cousin Agatha's. He left the apartment so fast that he didn't even notice that his favorite baseball glove had vanished.

CHAPTER ONE

Work in Progress

On clear mornings like this one, a satellite high over the outskirts of London would have detected a curiously perfect square of land with a lavender rectangle right in the middle. The estate below was laid out geometrically: the gardens, walkways, fountains, and the venerable Victorian mansion with its distinctive lavender roof.

This was Mistery House, the ancestral home of twelve-year-old Agatha and her eccentric family. Her parents spent very little time in London, breezing in for quick visits between trips to far-flung corners of the earth, often traveling for months at a time. As Agatha grew up, she became so comfortable with their comings and goings that she stopped even going to the airport to see them off. She preferred to stay at the mansion, making lists of all the projects she could tackle in their absence and getting to work as soon as she could.

During this trip, she'd decided to inventory and clean the Colonial Gallery.

"When was the last time we dusted in here?" Agatha asked the butler, Chandler, as she unlocked the heavy bolt.

Chandler shifted his weight, looking vaguely uncomfortable. "It must be at least a year, I should think, Miss."

"So long? And to think I used to explore it so often when I was a kid . . ."

"Mr. and Mrs. Mistery have never requested that I clean it," confessed the butler, a little embarrassed. "And I must admit that it had completely slipped my mind."

"It's better this way. Now there are even more things to rediscover," said Agatha happily, stroking the tip of her upturned nose. "Come on, let's go get our hands dirty!"

Her white Siberian cat, Watson, had already darted into the darkened room and was prowling from pillar to post, sniffing the assorted antiques. Armed with an enormous feather duster, Chandler strode across the threshold and went straight to the windows to let in some fresh air. A small breeze stirred up a thick cloud of dust. Luckily, the butler had come prepared, covering his immaculate dinner jacket with a protective layer.

The Colonial Gallery was located in the house's vast basement, and the ancient stones of the manor's foundations could be seen at points where the plaster had chipped away over the years. Like a museum exhibit, the hall was divided into sections, each dedicated to one of the Mistery family's celebrated ancestors. Over the centuries, each of them had gathered precious exotic relics from all corners of the globe and brought them back to London, where they were now stashed in cabinets and shelves or displayed on pedestals.

As soon as the dust had settled, Agatha walked across the room and looked around as though she were gazing at an enchanted palace. "Marvelous!" she whispered. "Why did I wait so long to come back down here?"

Her voice was full of regret. This part of the house was a treasure trove of curiosities. Agatha had a mind like a steel trap, and could effortlessly memorize details of anything that crossed her path. She spent her free time devouring books on all sorts of topics, and jotting down the most interesting facts in her trusty notebook. It was all part of her plan to become a world-famous mystery writer!

The butler tried to soothe her. "Mistery House is too big to keep tabs on every room . . . It's always hiding some new surprise!"

Agatha rubbed her hands together. "You're right, Chandler," she said with a smile. "Do you mind if I take a quick peek around while you get started cleaning?"

"Not at all, Miss."

Agatha approached the first pedestal. The bronze plaque bore the name Margaret Mistery. Agatha's great-aunt had been an intrepid anthropologist, specializing in musical instruments. She had collected Celtic harps, Egyptian lutes, Amazonian drums, and many other unusual instruments.

"This must be a didgeridoo," said Agatha, pointing at a five-foot-long hollow tube.

Chandler paused to shake out his feather duster, glancing at the unusual item. "Do you need a hand moving it?" he asked.

"Thanks. I'd like to get a closer look at the carvings."

"As you wish, Miss Agatha."

Chandler was a former heavyweight boxer, and he kept in shape with constant exercise. The massive didgeridoo seemed to weigh little more than a twig in his giant hands.

"If my memory serves me correctly, indigenous Australians carve these from huge eucalyptus branches that have been hollowed out by termites," Agatha said with excitement. "They paint them with traditional tribal colors and play them during ceremonies."

The butler nodded.

"Don't you think it's amazing?" Agatha asked him. "It's an antique, probably dating back to the Stone Age."

"It seems a bit unwieldy, to be honest," said Chandler. "How do you play such a thing?"

"You blow into it like a trombone and tap on

the tube to modulate the sound." Agatha was more and more engrossed. "Want to give it a try?"

Chandler brushed the instrument down with the feather duster, then put it to his mouth and blew as hard as he could.

A cloud of dust puffed out of the far end of the tube, covering Watson from head to tail. The cat jumped, startled, and fled to a corner to clean his fur.

"So sorry," Chandler apologized. "I didn't see him there."

The aspiring writer laughed heartily while moving on to the second pedestal, which displayed a huge wooden totem.

The plaque revealed the name Miles Mistery, translator of Native American languages during the English settlement of the New World. The Mohicans had taken a fancy to him and swamped him with all sorts of gifts from various tribes.

CHAPTER ONE

Agatha noticed a strange object hanging from the totem, a circle of bent wood hung with feathers and strips of deerskin. She recalled reading somewhere that they were called dream catchers, and that according to the Native Americans, they were used to encourage good dreams and rid the user of nightmares. She took out her notebook and pen, jotting down notes for a story.

"Okay, the first scene could begin like this . . . ," she muttered. "The settlers believe that the dream catchers are calling in evil spirits to frighten their herds away . . . a girl in the village discovers that it's really a band of greedy fur trappers, playing on their superstitions . . ." She continued to write for several minutes, while Chandler dusted and polished tirelessly. "That could work!" she exclaimed with satisfaction, closing her notebook and putting it back in her pocket.

Just then she heard a thud. In his wanderings, Watson had knocked over a large ebony mask found in sub-Saharan Africa by Frederick Mistery. Uncle Fred, as Agatha's mother called him, had been a celebrated ballet dancer. One day he'd decided to give up the stage and went to live among African tribes so that he could learn their dances. He had returned in a ship full of fascinating objects: statues, ritual staffs, spears, carved shields, and many other intriguing artifacts. The most precious of all was the scary-looking headdress Watson had bumped.

Agatha went to examine the carving. Maybe the giant mask would inspire a story. Chandler hurried over to help set it back in its place.

But Agatha seemed to have other ideas. "What do you say I try it on?" she asked.

"Are you sure, Miss?" replied the butler, taken aback. "It might be too heavy for you."

"It'll be fine if we knot the cords over my shoulders," the girl insisted.

Within minutes, Agatha was covered from head to toe by the African headdress. "I bet I look terrifying!" She laughed, stumbling blindly around the room.

"If Mistery House were infested with evil spirits, they would flee in terror," Chandler confirmed with the hint of a smile.

But it wasn't a ghost that was terrified . . .

"ARRRRRRGHHH!" someone screamed from the doorway.

Dash, who'd been searching all over the house for his cousin, had been drawn to the Colonial Gallery when he heard thumping noises downstairs. Now he was faced by this nightmare vision. He was ready to bolt when Agatha took off her disguise and did her utmost to calm him down.

"We need to fly to Venice in just over an hour!" announced Dash after he had composed himself.

"Are you ready for another mission?"

"Ready as always," replied Agatha, touching her nose. "I'll just need a minute to contact a relative. There must be a Mistery living in the most beautiful city in Italy!"

"And I'll need to repack our bags," added Chandler.

Agatha ran to her bedroom to consult her family tree—a giant globe marked with the locations, occupations, and relationships of all the Misterys, each accompanied by a photo. She made a quick phone call, tossed a few research books into the suitcase that Chandler had packed, and put Watson into his cat carrier.

She rejoined the others, announcing cheerfully, "Let's go to the *aeroporto*, dear colleagues. Next stop, Venice!"

CHAPTER TWO

The Most Serene

The flight from London to Venice was just two hours long. As soon as they'd fastened their seat belts for takeoff, Dash pulled out his EyeNet to run through the details of the case with the others.

"This is the doge's crown," he began, showing them a photo on the screen. "It belongs to a Mr. Alfredo Modigliani and his wife, Melissa. The theft occurred last night at their Venetian palazzo, after a meal with three wealthy friends. Since the guests are all important people, Mr. Modigliani has not yet reported the theft to the local police. But the company that insured the crown has a great deal of money at risk, so this morning they hired Eye International to find out who is responsible."

"So the client is not the victim of the theft, but the insurance company is," Agatha summarized. "That's quite unusual, don't you think?"

Dash and Chandler nodded.

"Unfortunately, that's not the only thing that's unusual," Dash went on. "Normally, Eye International sends me all the available files in the archives, but this time I've been told there'll be a delay."

"Very strange!" said Agatha. "What's in the files?"

"Biographical files on the three dinner guests, an architect's plan of Palazzo Modigliani, and basically everything else we'd need for a by-the-book investigation," snorted Dash.

Chandler cleared his throat. "Why the delay, Master Dash?"

"Some sort of technical glitch in the Eye International archives," the boy replied, rolling his eyes. "I bet I could fix it in ten minutes flat. They need a young brain." His face lit up with a hopeful smile. "That's where you come in, Agatha."

"Me?" Agatha was stunned. Dash, who loved anything high-tech, often teased her about her old-fashioned preference for books and paper maps. "How can I help?"

Dash patted her shoulder. "I'm betting that your famous memory drawers will come in handy," he said with a chuckle. "For starters, what is a doge?"

Agatha's precise response sounded as if she were quoting an encyclopedia. "The doge was the political leader of the Republic of Venice, back when Italy was divided into small city-states," she explained. "He was identified by a style of headgear known as the Corno Ducal, a

crownlike rim studded with precious stones and topped by a horn-shaped bonnet of gold or purple brocade."

Dash and Chandler listened to her lecture in awe. Even Watson stared up at his mistress from inside his cat carrier.

"Wait!" Agatha slapped her palm to her forehead. "I'm forgetting an important detail!"

"We're all ears, Miss," said Chandler, smoothing his cravat.

Agatha bit her lip and added dramatically, "Over the centuries, more than a hundred doges held this esteemed title in the Republic of Venice. Each had his own distinctive crown. This may or may not be relevant to our investigation, but if Mr. Modigliani had his own Corno Ducal, it's likely that he is of noble birth."

"Right you are," Dash confirmed. "The few details I managed to dig up online identified Mr. Modigliani as part of an ancient and wealthy house. The palazzo has belonged to his family for centuries."

"And probably needs expensive upkeep. Do you think he could have orchestrated a fake robbery to pocket the insurance money?" asked Chandler.

"It's entirely possible," replied Agatha. "But it's too early to say for sure."

"No worries," said Dash. "As soon as I lay eyes on his face, I'll be able to tell if he's the culprit!" The others looked puzzled, until the young detective explained the concept of criminal physiognomy. He leaned back in his airplane seat, looking smug. "I'm kind of an expert on the subject," he boasted.

In truth, he knew a lot more about battling

alien monsters, but he kept that detail to himself.

"Are there any more facts that might help with the case?" asked Chandler.

Agatha gave them a quick recap of Venice's history. "For centuries, the Most Serene Republic of Venice was a great maritime power with a fleet that dominated the Mediterranean and traded riches with the Orient," she recalled. "Its unique charms still attract millions of tourists each year."

"What's so special about it?" asked Dash, who knew even less about geography than he did about criminal physiognomy.

Agatha pulled a map of Venice out of her bag and laid it across their laps. "What do you notice?"

Dash shrugged. "Why are all the streets blue?"

"Because they're not streets, dear cousin! The city is built entirely on water," she said, passing a finger over the map. "There are no cars or trucks. The buildings are surrounded by a network of canals that can be traversed only by boat."

"The famous gondolas?" Dash asked. "Those long boats that cousin Marco pilots?"

Agatha nodded. She had confirmed their relative's profession during the short phone call she'd made to him before they left London. Marco Misterioso was a third cousin, part of the Italian branch of the Mistery family.

Chandler cleared his throat and said, "That reminds me. I seem to recall something about Cousin Marco being unable to pick us up at the airport?"

"That's right," said Agatha. "He was very sorry, but it's Carnevale and the city is packed with tourists. We're going to meet him in the Piazza San Marco, also called St. Mark's Square."

Dash was checking the map when his EyeNet suddenly let out a series of very loud *BLIPS!*

The passengers across the aisle turned to glare at him.

"I forgot to lower the volume on my computer

game," Dash apologized, punching at keys. "I'll make it shut up now, I swear!"

He managed to turn off the sound just as a list of files popped onto the screen. "Agatha, it's the information we're waiting for!" he exclaimed, pumping his fist in the air in victory. "We can finally get started."

"Too bad we're ready to land, dear cousin," she smiled, grasping the armrests.

The plane landed smoothly on the runway and within a short time they were walking along the corridor with their luggage. The airport was crowded with tourists from all over the world, coming to join in the masked balls and citywide party of Carnevale. Despite the chaos, they were able to board a passenger bus to the Grand Canal.

Agatha was right, thought Dash—Venice was a city beyond comparison. The boats gliding on the aqua canals, the buildings that seemed to sprout right out of the water, the arching footbridges, and the colorful stalls with traditional masks would be etched in his memory forever.

They boarded a *vaporetto*, a ferrylike water bus that rocked under their feet and made Chandler and Watson a little uneasy. During the trip, the aspiring detectives tried to review the files and exchange opinions, but they were distracted by the spectacular ride up the Grand Canal. When they got off at the marble steps at Piazza San Marco, flanked by a statue of St. Theodore and a tall column topped by a winged lion, Agatha gasped at the dreamlike beauty before her eyes. Pigeons wheeled over the busy square, past a tall clock tower and the white wedding-cake domes of St. Mark's Basilica. A medieval archway led into the maze of shopping streets called the Rialto, which was full of tourists with shopping bags and kids licking cones of brightly colored gelato.

Agatha noticed a young, curly-haired man with a cheerful face and a jaunty grin heading toward them through the crowd. He wore a traditional gondolier's shirt with black-and-white stripes, and his upper arms were the size of hams.

"Marco!" she shouted, cupping her hands around her mouth. "We're over here!"

Their cousin rushed over, raising a storm of pigeons. "It's great to see my English cousins!" he said, giving a low bow.

Agatha and her companions had agreed in advance, as always, not to disclose any more than they had to about Dash's mission. After an exchange of warm greetings, Agatha told Marco their cover story. "We're here to celebrate

Carnevale, but we're dizzy with wonder at Venice's beauty!"

Marco beamed proudly. "I'm at your disposal," he announced, pounding a fist on his chest. "I'll take you to see all the most picturesque corners of the city, all from a truly unique perspective: the seats of my gondola!"

"Perfect!" said Dash. "Let's start with Palazzo Modigliani!"

"Why do you want to go there?" Marco asked. "Just between us, it's not really one of the hot spots."

"The Modiglianis are friends of the family," lied Agatha, who did not want to get caught up in long explanations. "My parents asked me to drop by as soon as we arrived in town."

"Very good, then!" Marco led the group to the edge of the Grand Canal, where a small fleet of gondolas bobbed in the water, and pointing one out, he said, "Here is my magical boat. Isn't it the most beautiful one of them all?"

"Are you sure it will hold my weight?" Chandler asked hesitantly.

Smiling, the young man helped Chandler on board, with Agatha and Dash close behind. Marco then positioned himself at the stern, maneuvering the long oar with skill. In a booming voice, he began singing the melody of an ancient Venetian boat song as he propelled them along the canal.

It seemed like only a few moments before the stern profile of Palazzo Modigliani appeared before their eager eyes.

CHAPTER THREE

A Word with the Suspects

Palazzo Modigliani was a three-story stucco building covered in tangles of ivy. The ancient wrought-iron gate sat directly on the canal alongside a small boat dock.

"Come on, hurry up!" urged Dash, jumping out of the gondola before it was moored. He promptly slipped on the wet stones and almost fell into the water. Thanks to highly trained reflexes, Chandler quickly grabbed him and helped him back onto the dock.

"Th-that was close . . . ," stammered the young detective. "I almost became fish food!"

CHAPTER THREE

"Dash, there aren't any piranhas in Venice," laughed Agatha.

Then she turned to Marco. "Would you mind waiting for us? We might be a while."

"No problem. I kept my whole afternoon free for you," said the gondolier, breaking into another loud song.

Taking the lead, Agatha glanced at the doorbell. The Modiglianis lived on the top floors of the mansion, while the ground floor was a vacant office. She noticed the front gate was broken and beckoned to her companions to follow her into the lobby.

"How do you want to proceed?" she asked Dash quietly. "You said all three suspects are waiting for us, right?"

"Eye International has gathered them all together so we can reconstruct what happened," replied Dash, checking his time on his EyeNet. "It's three o'clock. We're right on the dot."

"Have you both memorized the suspects' files?" Agatha asked.

"Of course, Miss," replied Chandler.

Dash had already mounted the stairs, taking them three at a time. He pushed the bell and the door was opened by an enormous butler. He looked as if he'd been carved out of marble, and was dressed in the with impeccable style as Chandler.

"Ahhhh!" Dash cried. "You could be twins! Separated at birth!"

Behind him, Chandler raised an eyebrow in astonishment.

CHAPTER THREE

"May I help you?" asked the manservant, impassive.

Agatha moved forward. "The insurance company sent us to investigate the theft of the doge's crown," she said politely.

The butler moved to let them pass. "Signor and Signora Modigliani are waiting for you in the parlor."

Five people sat in the room they entered: the two Modiglianis and their three dinner guests from the night before. Agatha recognized them from the photos on the EyeNet.

Baron von Horvath from Hungary was short and plump with bushy gray sideburns. His file described him as a ruthless collector of antiquities, with no qualms about breaking the law to obtain a particular object that caught his interest.

The Englishman, Lord Cedric Spencer Edwards, was tall and reedy with an aristocratic bearing and a pencil-thin mustache. He was known to have a weakness for gambling.

The last guest was a handsome young Spaniard. Gonzago Suárez y Acevedo was in his thirties, the wealthy son of a famous bullfighter.

"Who are these young people, Nunzio?" asked Mr. Modigliani, turning to his butler.

"The insurance company's investigators, sir."

"How can that be?" he asked, bristling with irritation. "Two kids and a cat?"

Melissa Modigliani spoke up from her armchair at the far end of the room. "I'd imagine the detective is the robust fellow behind them, my dear," she said.

"You've hit the nail on the head," said Agatha with a little smile. "Allow me to introduce the infallible detective DM14. My cousin Dash and I are his assistants."

"Precisely," agreed the large butler, moving to shake hands with everybody.

CHAPTER THREE

Dash elbowed Agatha and whispered, "Check out Mr. Modigliani. His eyes are beady and too close together. According to the rules of criminal physiognomy, he's hiding something. I just know he's the guilty party!"

Before Agatha could reply, the Hungarian, Baron von Horvath, jumped to his feet.

"Can we get a move on?" he demanded, glaring at Chandler. "I'm a very busy man and I can't afford to spend the rest of the day here!"

"Understood," smiled Agatha. "Why don't you each tell Agent DM14 what happened here last night?"

Alfredo Modigliani began to speak in somber tones. "As you're aware, a precious family heirloom was stolen from my study. These gentlemen were invited for dinner at eight, but I don't hold any of them responsible for the theft. Clearly whoever it was came in through the window."

CHAPTER THREE

"We'll establish all that in time," said Agatha, a flash of cleverness lighting her eyes. "The insurance company wants to be very clear on exactly what happened, so you're all considered suspects until proven otherwise."

"How dare you, young lady!" cried the English lord in indignation. "To cast aspersions on a member of the great house of Edwards! We are not common thieves!"

Baron von Horvath muttered under his breath and lit a cigar.

Only the Spaniard, Gonzago, sat calmly in place, as though Agatha's provocation did not concern him in the slightest.

"Go on, Mr. Modigliani," Chandler said. "What was the first thing that happened at your dinner party?"

Casting a nervous glance at his wife, Alfredo Modigliani continued to speak. "I wanted to show the doge's crown to my distinguished guests," he said, hesitating. "We had been in the study for only a few minutes, and I had just taken it out of the safe when Nunzio announced that dinner was served. So I left the crown on my desk and accompanied my guests to the dining room immediately." His wife shot him a look, and he added, "My darling Melissa doesn't like it when the soup isn't piping hot . . ."

"Were you all together throughout the dinner?" Chandler asked.

"Absolutely," confirmed Modigliani. "That includes Nunzio, who served his delicious specialties: risotto with lagoon shrimp, liver alla veneziana, and of course some *fritelle,* the traditional Carnevale pastries. We stayed at the table until ten o'clock."

Agatha carefully noted the time in her notebook. "And then what happened?" she asked without raising her head from the page.

This time Gonzago was first to respond. "I

had just arrived from Spain yesterday afternoon, so I was very tired. I excused myself and took a water taxi back to my hotel."

"I can assure you he's telling the truth. I accompanied him to the door myself," confirmed Mrs. Modigliani. "Then I went to bed as well. I had a very bad headache."

"I went to the parlor to make a private phone call," explained Lord Edwards.

"Baron von Horvath and I," continued Modigliani, "continued to chat while Nunzio cleared away the dishes. And then . . ."

"Let me go first, if you don't mind," interrupted the Hungarian nobleman. "I could not find my cigars, so I asked Mr. Modigliani's permission to go back to his study, where I was sure I had left them. That's when a strange thing happened . . ."

"What?" asked Agatha and Dash in unison.

"I couldn't find the right room. I was certain

I knew where it was, but I opened the door to a different room. So I returned to the dining room to tell Alfredo about my confusion."

"At which point," continued Modigliani, "I went to get his cigars myself. But as soon as I entered the study, I found the window wide open, and the crown was gone! Clearly, someone must have climbed the outside wall and come in through the window."

Agatha rubbed her chin. "But it's also true that each one of you, at some point after dinner, had the opportunity to go to the study alone."

Lord Edwards let out another enraged outburst and Dash took the opportunity to move closer to Agatha. "Watch out, he has sharp cheekbones," he whispered. "According to physiognomy, that means he's a violent man!"

Agatha wasn't impressed. "Could you please tell us whom you called, Lord Edwards?"

"That's none of your business!" he snapped.

CHAPTER THREE

"Perhaps it would be easier if you calmed down," said Gonzago with a charming smile.

Agatha saw Melissa Modigliani cast a glance at the young Spaniard. Agatha didn't need to be a physiognomy expert to sense that there was a strange understanding between the two. She turned her attention back to Baron von Horvath. "You say you were unable to find the study," she noted, "even though you'd been in it right before dinner."

Increasingly nervous, the Hungarian noble replied that he'd gone down the dark hallway that he thought led to the study. But when he opened the door, he'd seen a suit of armor where he remembered there being a fireplace.

"My ancestors collected historical armor," said Mr. Modigliani. "There are several examples in the house. The baron went to the wrong room."

In the silence that followed, Dash drew

Agatha and Chandler aside. "This is really a tricky one." He sighed.

"I think we've seen the worst of it," said the butler, nodding.

"So what do we do now?"

As usual, Agatha had an idea. "Mr. Modigliani, would you please show us your study?" she asked.

CHAPTER FOUR
On the Clue Trail

As soon as Modigliani opened the door to his study, the detectives saw the marble fireplace directly in front of them. To its left, a wooden bookcase stretched up to the ceiling, divided in two by a floor-length mirror. On the opposite side sat a mahogany desk cluttered with pens, inkwells, and monogrammed stationery. There was a window above it.

"That's the window the thief must have used," Dash said, rushing toward it.

Chandler moved to the right of the door to examine a suit of Byzantine armor.

"Where is the safe you mentioned to us

earlier?" Agatha asked Mr. Modigliani.

He pulled some books from a low shelf, revealing a secret panel with a combination lock. Pressing a complicated series of numbers, he swung the door open, revealing a small hidden safe. "The crown was kept here," he whispered, pointing to an empty space. "I was such a fool! I should have put it back safely before we all went to the dining room. But who could have imagined such a thing would happen?"

Agatha was beginning to think that Mr. Modigliani had made a few too many mistakes. "Was the window closed?" she asked.

He nodded in despair. "I was the last one to leave the room, and I'm sure none of my guests opened the window while I was unlocking the safe."

"What other clues are there?" Agatha pressed. "Did you see any signs that someone had climbed in?"

CHAPTER FOUR

"Nothing," said Mr. Modigliani softly. "As soon as I noticed the theft, I closed the shutters and called the insurance company. I didn't touch anything."

"Good," said Chandler, who had been listening to the whole conversation with rapt attention. "Now, could you please leave us alone for a few minutes?"

Mr. Modigliani left the study without another word. The three investigators remained, listening to his footsteps fade as he walked down the hall. Then they began to speak.

"Did you find anything?" Agatha began.

"Judging by the dust, the armor hasn't been moved in a long time," said Chandler. "It's likely that Baron von Horvath really did try the wrong room."

Dash looked out the window. "The side of the building is covered in vines, roof to ground."

"So if the thief were agile, he could easily have

climbed up two floors or come down from the roof, and disappeared with the loot," observed Agatha, stroking the tip of her nose. "Even the leaves confirm this theory . . ."

"What leaves?" asked Dash, astounded.

Agatha pointed at Watson, who was playing under the desk. She knelt down and retrieved two dark green leaves. "Don't you know ivy is poisonous, darling?" she asked the cat.

Watson gave her an offended look and went to find something else to amuse himself.

CHAPTER FOUR

"Maybe the wind blew these inside," said Agatha, showing the others the leaves. "But we still haven't addressed the fundamental problem."

"What's that?" asked Dash, scratching his head.

Chandler responded first. "If the thief came in through the window, he must have had help from somebody inside the house," he stated.

"Why? Couldn't he have just picked the lock on the window and let himself in?"

Agatha gave him a smile. "Ask yourself: How would he know that the crown had been left on the desk unattended?" she asked.

"Of course!" Dash exclaimed. "That's true!"

"In fact, the open window could very well be a false clue to throw us off the track," Agatha mused aloud.

"So what's our next step?"

"Simple," she replied, tapping her nose with

her finger. "In either case, someone inside the house must be involved, so we should follow our suspects' next steps. The question is, who do we trail first? I wish we could follow them all at once!"

Dash brightened. "Agatha, you're a genius—we can use the biometric scanner!"

The others stared in silence as Dash explained that his EyeNet had been fitted with a new app. The biometric scanner recorded a person's body imprint: blood circulation, heartbeat, nervous system, and other vital signs. Once the data was entered, thanks to GPS satellites, it was possible to track a person's movements online.

"Perfect!" Agatha rejoiced. "We'll scan all our suspects, then start shadowing their every move. We just have to do it without getting caught!"

They rejoined Modigliani and his guests in the parlor. While Chandler told them that the evidence suggested that another person had entered the study through the window, scattering ivy leaves in the process, Dash took advantage of Chandler's huge frame to record the biometric values of everyone in the room on his EyeNet without being seen.

When he signaled that he had finished, Agatha collected the guests' cell-phone numbers, assuring them they'd be informed of the progress of their investigation.

The three gentlemen left Palazzo Modigliani quickly, each in a hurry to return to his usual occupation.

"How do you plan to proceed, Agent DM14?" asked Melissa. "Do you have clues to follow?"

Caught off guard, Chandler started to twist his cravat.

"He can't tell you anything yet," Agatha jumped in, rescuing him with a clever smile. "But we can assure you the thief will be caught very soon."

"Excellent!" said Mr. Modigliani.

Even Nunzio stopped dusting for a moment to observe them with approval.

Agatha and the others took their leave and returned to Marco, who was humming to himself in his gondola.

"Nice long visit," he said with a smile. "Are you ready for your tour?"

Dash was watching three blinking lights as they moved across the EyeNet's screen. Von Horvath was definitely the closest. Agatha looked at the Hungarian baron's position and made a decision. "Let's head toward the Blacksmith Canal," she suggested.

"Aha, then you want to visit the workshops!" cried Marco, enthusiastically grabbing the long oar. "Come on, off we go!"

They boarded the gondola and the young Venetian steered them through a maze of canals, passing under footbridges and gliding

past beautiful buildings. There were boats everywhere, some delivering vegetables and fresh fish to the markets.

Dash kept his eyes glued to the EyeNet throughout the whole trip, and Marco continued to sing like a nightingale. After about twenty minutes, they tied up at a dock and immediately started to search for their target. It seemed the baron had gone into an antique store.

Dash peered through the window and saw the stocky von Horvath handing a wrapped package to the proprietor, a toothless old man with a grim frown.

"Aha!" cried the young detective, snapping his fingers. "The baron's chubby cheeks should have made me suspect him from the very beginning!"

"Why is that?" asked Agatha.

"According to criminal physiognomy, they're a sign of moral weakness. But . . . watch out! He's coming back out—hide!"

CHAPTER FOUR

Von Horvath left the store, looking over his shoulder suspiciously. Agatha scooped up Watson and slipped into a souvenir shop, while Dash ducked behind a large planter. Chandler opened a newspaper, hiding his face. Only Marco remained in full view.

"Okay, kids, what just happened?" Marco asked as soon as the Hungarian had turned the corner. "What's with all the subterfuge?"

With no other option, Agatha confessed the real reason for their trip to Venice. "And if I can't retrieve the doge's crown, I'll flunk the mission," Dash added bitterly.

Marco was delighted. "You should have told me sooner," he declared. "I love a good spy story!"

The only thing left to do was come up with a plan.

"While Marco keeps watch and Chandler distracts the antiques dealer, Dash and I will try to get a look at the package the baron left," Agatha said.

"As you wish, Miss," agreed Chandler.

They entered the store as if they were typical English tourists. Dash leafed through Agatha's guidebook as Chandler began speaking in clumsy Italian to the old shopkeeper, who stood rubbing his bony hands together.

"My mother might like a Murano glass ornament," said Agatha in a perky voice to Chandler. Her quick eye had noticed a shelf of them at the far end of the shop.

"Yes," Chandler replied, turning to the shopkeeper. "Could you help me choose one?"

"Of course, of course, excellent choice," said the antiques dealer. "Right this way, sir."

As Chandler and the shopkeeper walked away, Dash snatched von Horvath's package from behind the counter. Unwrapping it quickly, he found an old wooden box. Could the crown be inside it?

CHAPTER FOUR

"Go on, open it!" Agatha encouraged him in a sidelong whisper.

Dash began wrestling with the rusty clasp. Suddenly, the box slipped out his fingers and landed on a case of glass beads.

The noise alerted the shopkeeper. "What are you doing?" he shouted. "Get out of my shop, you clumsy brats!"

The three Londoners left in a hurry. But before they escaped completely, Agatha turned back to see the shopkeeper pick up the contents of the upturned box: an antique Arabian dagger with a curved blade.

They had caused all that commotion for nothing!

CHAPTER FIVE

Hot Pursuit by Gondola

"Von Horvath was a big waste of time," said Dash, disappointed, as they trooped back to Marco's gondola.

"He sure was," agreed Agatha. "But don't give up. We have two more suspects to tail."

At that exact moment, the EyeNet's screen started blinking. Dash pushed a series of buttons and Lord Edwards's movements appeared.

"He's not far away!" Dash exclaimed. "Look at this."

Within minutes, Marco had skillfully directed them to Campo San Zaccaria, which was swarming with people in swirling capes and feathered headdresses. It was a beautiful sight, but there was no time for them to admire the masked revelers and their festivities.

"Over there! No, there!" Dash's voice echoed through the twisting alleys.

After a few laps around the square, they finally located Lord Edwards. He stood under a large stone archway talking to a man in a long cloak and pearly white mask.

"The masked man has a package tucked under his arm; can you see it?" Agatha sounded excited. "He could be our thief! Let's get closer."

The crowd was so dense it was hard to maneuver. Using his massive frame, Chandler led the group through the throng. As they approached the stone archway, the mysterious man lowered his mask.

"Hey, I know him!" exclaimed Marco. "That's Calindo Freddi. He's a slippery one!"

Right at that moment, Calindo turned toward

them. He caught sight of Chandler's imposing form heading toward him, whispered something to the Englishman, and ducked quickly into the crowd, doing his best to vanish.

"Follow that masked man!" shouted Dash. "The crown is inside that package, I'm sure of it!"

Chandler elbowed his way through the crowd, with Dash and Agatha hot on his heels. But Calindo had a good head start. He jumped into a small boat on the canal, threw off the mooring rope, and began paddling away furiously.

"This way!" cried Marco. He grabbed hold of a fellow gondolier and, after a brief exchange in Italian, turned back to the group. "My friend Nicola is lending us his gondola," he told them. "Get on board!"

In a matter of moments, they were in hot pursuit.

"Can't we go any faster?" Dash despaired. "This must be the world's slowest chase!"

CHAPTER FIVE

"I'm afraid not. Gondolas are delicate, so if I'm not careful, we could damage Nicola's boat."

Calindo's small boat was faster, but less stable, which meant he had to slow down to avoid getting swamped by a passing *vaporetto*. But somehow the distance between the two boats never seemed to change.

"Come on, Marco. Can't we get closer?" yelled Agatha.

Every so often, Calindo turned to look over his shoulder. He had freed himself from the mask and cloak in order to move more easily.

The chase continued for several more minutes. Then the canal split into two smaller streams and Calindo, after a moment of indecision, took the left.

Marco, on the other hand, steered to the right.

"Hey, what are you doing?" yelled Dash.

"Don't worry," Marco replied. "Calindo has trapped himself!"

"Of course," said Agatha. "This canal is a shortcut. We'll be able to cut him off up ahead!"

Marco stared at her. "How did you know that?" he asked.

"I memorized the canal map," she replied. "I thought it might come in handy!"

"Your memory drawers are overflowing as ever, Miss Agatha," said Chandler, smiling.

There were no other boats on the small canal Marco had taken. He slowed his gondola, telling the others that they had arrived at the point where their canal intersected with Calindo Freddi's.

They jumped onto a narrow path running alongside the waterway and hid behind a corner until Agatha spied Calindo's boat moving in their direction. They were all flattened against the wall when the sound of lapping water announced the arrival of their prey. Chandler reached out a long arm and grabbed Calindo by the collar of his jacket.

"Rats!" cursed Calindo. "Let go of me!"

It was a funny sight, the man squirming and kicking his legs in midair as the mighty butler hoisted him up to the path.

"What's the idea? Put me down!"

Chandler shrugged. "All right." He let go and the man fell on his backside in the middle of the group.

"Confess everything!" said Dash, pointing his finger at him.

"Who are you?" replied Calindo. "Leave me alone, or I'll call the police!"

"Go right ahead," said Agatha. "I'm sure they'd like to hear a few things from you."

"Hear what? I haven't done a thing!" Calindo protested loudly, hoping to catch the attention of passersby.

"That's what every criminal says." Dash folded his arms.

"I'm not a criminal. Let me go!"

CHAPTER FIVE

Calindo tried to stand up, but Chandler pinned him in place with a giant hand on his shoulder.

Agatha wanted to find out why he had been meeting with Lord Edwards. She began to bombard him with questions, but he just stared at the ground.

"It would be in your best interest to start talking," Marco warned. "Everybody in Venice knows you've always got your hands in somebody's pockets."

Calindo Freddi refused to respond.

Agatha tried persuading him with a clever deception. "Lord Edwards is in big trouble with the law," she cautioned him. "If you give us information, I promise we'll let you go."

Calindo looked at each of them, then gave up with a sigh.

"That Edwards guy, he's got a bit of a gambling problem," he said. "He'll put good money on anything—horse races, football games, race cars. I carry money from respectable gents like him so they don't have to get their hands dirty."

Dash narrowed his eyes. "Yeah, I can just imagine the sort of people you're dealing with . . ."

"Where were you last night?" Agatha interrupted, careful not to mince words. "And don't try to lie to me!"

Calindo threw his arms wide, doing his best to look innocent. "At the Venice Casino," he admitted. "I had to play roulette on behalf of some of my . . . um . . . clients. There were dozens of witnesses; you can ask anyone who was there."

"We will," Agatha promised. "And who were these, um . . . clients?"

"Well, one was Lord Fitz. He called me at ten o'clock to ask me to bet for him."

"That's exactly when Edwards claims he stepped out to make his private phone call," mused Agatha under her breath. "The one that was none of our business."

"And then?" Dash continued.

"I stayed at the casino till closing time, then I bought myself a gelato. Pistachio. This morning I called Edwards to set up a meeting. I had to give him his winnings." He pulled the package out of his pocket and opened it to reveal a fat pile of banknotes. "He asked me to put everything down on seven. I swear, never in my life have I met such a lucky guy. Seven came up three times in a row!"

Chandler pulled him up from the ground as though he weighed nothing at all. "So why were you in a disguise today?"

"Hey, it's Carnevale. Plus, a guy in my line of work needs to keep a low profile," replied Calindo with a crooked smile. He was beginning to regain his confidence. "Can I go now?"

Agatha nodded, but kept her serious

expression. "Go on," she said. "But if we discover that you've told us a pack of lies, we'll advise the police."

"Don't worry, Miss." Calindo grinned. "Ask around. I'm a trustworthy guy." He gave them an exaggerated bow, jumped into his boat, and rowed away without looking back.

"Do you believe him, Agatha?" Dash asked.

"His alibi should be easy enough to verify," she replied. "Every roulette dealer at the casino would remember him winning on sevens three times in a row."

"You're right," grumbled Dash. "So now what?"

"I think it's about time we spoke with Gonzago," she said. "Where does the EyeNet say he is now?"

Dash looked at the screen. "Oh!" he cried.

"What's the matter?

"The EyeNet says he's in a hotel overlooking

Piazza San Marco. But . . ."

"But what?" Marco urged him. "Don't just leave us hanging!"

"Well . . . there's another signal . . . I mean, another suspect is with him!"

"Who?" asked Agatha.

Chandler peered over Dash's shoulder. "Looks like Mrs. Modigliani."

"Incredible!" exclaimed Agatha, startled by this turn of events. "What are we waiting for? Let's join them!"

CHAPTER SIX

Family Secrets

The waterways were lit up by the pastel and gold colors of sunset. In the winding streets, lamplights glowed like lost fireflies.

"I'm an idiot," Dash muttered as they hurried back to the square. "I should have suspected the Spaniard long before now!"

"Because of his chin, or some other criminal physiognomy clue?" asked Agatha in a sarcastic tone.

"Too handsome," her cousin replied. "And anybody who comes off so calm and polite must have something to hide!"

Agatha sighed. "I'm going to have to clear

up a few things for you when we get back to London."

"You'll see! He's the culprit." Dash had no doubt about it. "Don't you get it? He's with Mrs. Modigliani right now. They must be accomplices. After all, she was the one who showed him to the door last night—maybe they made a quick stop at her husband's study first."

Marco moored the borrowed gondola next to the Palazzo Ducale. The gothic building with its inlaid columns bore silent testament to a wealthy and powerful past, when Venice was the undisputed queen of the Mediterranean.

The streets were crowded to capacity. Dozens of masked people celebrated Carnevale, dancing to Renaissance music.

Chin down, Dash hunched over his EyeNet. A teenage girl peeled off from a noisy group, approaching the young detective. Dressed in a bell-shaped blue skirt and elbow-length gloves, she looked like a lovely, slightly punked-out Cinderella.

"That is so cool! Can I see it? I love technology!" the girl said, pointing to the EyeNet.

"Umm . . . you won't be able to use it," Dash lied quickly. "It's a next-generation device and it's programmed to work only with my fingerprints."

CHAPTER SIX

"Awesome! What is it? A tablet?"

"Uh . . . well, no . . . it's an HD videocamera. I have to film Carnevale celebrations for a school project."

"Really? Well, stop taking selfies! Why don't you film me?" She did a pirouette, making her blue skirt flare out. She was very pretty, and Dash couldn't help grinning. "Listen, I'm going to a party with my friends over there. They'd love to meet a film student with a titanium camera and cute British accent. Why don't you join us?"

"Umm . . . I can't," Dash mumbled. "I have to go . . ."

"What?" the girl interrupted, pouting. "You're going to leave a nice girl like me by herself and miss out on a supercool party? Are you nuts?"

"Yes . . . that is to say, no . . . excuse me, it's just . . . ," Dash babbled.

Cinderella stalked away in disappointment, not even bothering to look back.

"You're a real heartbreaker, little cousin," said Marco with a grin.

The young detective flushed as red as a lobster.

"Dash, focus. Where is Gonzago?" Agatha prompted him.

"He's right here," Dash replied. "At the Grand Hotel Transatlantic."

The sign above the hotel entrance was a huge golden anchor lit up with neon. The doorman's coat was studded with gold buttons and striped epaulets, like an admiral's uniform.

"Let's go in," said Agatha.

The fake naval officer intercepted them as they crossed the threshold. "May I help you with something?" he asked, eyeing Chandler, Watson, and Dash.

"We're meeting a friend who's staying here," replied Agatha.

"Very well. Go in and ask at the reception desk." From his tone of voice, it was clear that he was not entirely convinced by the girl's explanation.

The hotel lobby was decorated in the style of a sailing ship from long ago, with overstuffed club chairs, wood-paneled walls, sextants, and old nautical maps. The reception desk was equipped with brass instrument dials like a ship.

The hotel concierge, in her neat white officer's uniform, greeted them politely, asking what brought them to the hotel.

"We're friends of Mr. Gonzago Suárez y Acevedo," Agatha replied promptly. "Could you please tell us his room number?"

"I'm sorry, but Mr. Suárez explicitly asked not to be disturbed. If you would like, I can show you to the visitor's lounge and you can wait for him there."

"What should we do?" Dash asked his cousin as they stepped away from the desk. "We need to find out what he's up to!"

Agatha stroked her nose. "I have an idea," she said. "Listen carefully!" And she explained her plan in a whisper.

They followed the concierge to the visitor's lounge. Moments later, Chandler, with Watson tucked under his arm, strolled past the grand staircase that led up to the hotel rooms. As he neared the bottom step, the butler gave the white Siberian cat a small push, and Watson meowed and zoomed up the stairs.

"My cat!" cried Agatha, launching herself in pursuit.

"Her cat!" shouted Dash, right behind her. "Where are we going?" he hissed at his cousin.

"Room 312," said Agatha, racing upstairs after Watson.

"How do you know?" asked Dash, sprinting past her.

"I took a peek at the register while we were at the reception desk. Simple, right?"

CHAPTER SIX

They were at Gonzago's door in a flash. Watson was the first to arrive, guided by his feline instincts. Agatha took him in her arms and gave him a pat. "Good kitty," she whispered.

Dash put his ear to the door. He could clearly hear two voices engaged in a heated discussion. The blinking lights on the EyeNet confirmed the presence of Gonzago and Melissa Modigliani.

"How do we get inside?" Dash asked his cousin.

"Leave it to me." Agatha knocked softly on the door. An irritated voice from inside asked who it was. "Room service, sir."

A few seconds later, the door opened.

"But I didn't order anythi—"

Gonzago fell silent.

"Caught in the act!" cried Dash. He strode boldly through the door.

Sitting on the edge of the bed, Mrs. Modigliani gazed at the children in astonishment. A frenetic patter of footsteps announced the arrival of the concierge. She burst into the room as though the devil were chasing her.

"Mr. Suárez! Mr. Suárez! Some young pickpockets are on the loose in the hotel!" She stopped when she saw Dash and Agatha. "There you are! Don't worry, sir, I'll take care of this situation personally."

"Leave them be," said the Spaniard. "They're friends. Thank you for your concern, but you can go back to work now."

The concierge excused herself, throwing a furious look at Dash. The boy responded with his own well-practiced smirk.

"Mr. Suárez," Agatha began. "Perhaps you had better explain what's going on. This whole business looks highly suspicious."

The Spaniard ran a hand through his glossy hair. "Melissa, my dear," he said, turning to her. "I think the time has come to reveal the whole story."

CHAPTER SIX

"Aha! I knew there was something fishy going on!" exclaimed Dash.

Gonzago let out a sigh and went to sit beside Mrs. Modigliani on the bed. "You see, Melissa is my half sister," he said calmly.

Dash's jaw dropped. Chandler raised an eyebrow.

"The story goes back many years," explained the Spaniard. "My father was at the pinnacle of his bull-fighting career when he became engaged to a beautiful Italian lady, but he left her soon after the birth of their only daughter, Melissa."

Melissa looked down at the floor while Gonzago continued his tale. "Melissa's mother didn't want him to have any contact with the infant he left." He paused for a moment, gazing pensively out the window at the canal. He seemed to be searching for the right words. "Now my father is very sick, and he told me his story because he hoped to see his daughter again.

So I tracked Melissa down and came to Venice to meet her. It's such a wonderful thing to know I have a new sister." The Spaniard rested his hand on Melissa's shoulder with affection.

"Gonzago arrived yesterday," she confirmed. "We met in the afternoon and he asked if I would accompany him back to Spain to meet my father at last. I didn't know what to do. I have to confess, my husband knows nothing about any of this."

CHAPTER SIX

"Why such secrecy?" asked Agatha.

"My mother remarried when I was a baby. It would be such a blow to my husband to find out that I don't really come from a prominent Venetian lineage, as he has always believed," she replied. "But in the end I decided that I had to meet my birth father. I invited Gonzago to dinner so we could both tell him together."

"But there wasn't a good opportunity, because Lord Edwards and Baron von Horvath were there as well. Am I right?" Agatha guessed.

"Exactly. I didn't know the others were coming until the last minute. Gonzago and I chose to postpone the discussion, and met here today to decide our next step."

Chandler cleared his throat. "So your secret has nothing to do with the theft of the crown?" he asked bluntly.

"Absolutely not!" they replied in chorus.

They seemed sincere, preoccupied with

solving their own knotty problem.

Agatha thought for a moment, then whispered into Dash's ear. "They can each confirm the other's alibi. Let's apologize for the disturbance and wish them both luck."

So that's what they did, filing out of the room in disappointment. The case of the stolen crown was still far from solved.

CHAPTER SEVEN

Unexpected Help

The group left the Grand Hotel Transatlantic and stepped out into the Venetian evening.

Music and laughter sounded from all directions. The atmosphere of Carnevale spread through every street.

Marco said his farewells and went to return the borrowed gondola to his friend Nicola. The others stopped for a quick meal at a trattoria. Perched on a stool, Agatha reflected on the events of the previous night and the discoveries they had made that afternoon.

"There's nobody left," Dash said glumly, twirling a forkful of thick spaghetti as Agatha pondered in silence. "Do you think Nunzio might be able to give us a hand?"

"Actually, he's the one person we haven't questioned yet," offered Chandler between bites of cutlet. "I can assure you that servants always know what's going on in the household."

A smile appeared on Agatha's face. "That sounds like a good idea," she agreed, feeding Watson a bite of her fish. "But what should we ask him?"

"It's obvious!" said Dash. "The thief is Mr. Modigliani. He hid the crown so he could claim the insurance money, just as we suspected at the beginning. It's a classic crime."

"Too simple," replied his cousin. "If you ask me, we're overlooking a conspicuous detail."

"What's that?"

"The only way to find out is to go back to Palazzo Modigliani."

And so they resumed their investigation. The

streetlights reflected in the canals were enchanting, even if no one in the party was in the right state of mind for sightseeing.

At eight o'clock they spotted the windows of Palazzo Modigliani. The ancient building seemed to want to hide under cover of darkness. They asked a boatman for a ride, and disembarked once again on the dock in front of the entrance. The gate was still broken, so they decided to go upstairs without ringing the bell to announce themselves first. The stairway lights were not on, so the shadowy climb was more difficult than expected.

When they knocked on the door, Nunzio's usually impassive face greeted them with a stunned expression.

"Shall I announce you?" he asked.

"No, Nunzio," whispered Agatha. "We're here because we'd like to have a quick chat with you in Mr. Modigliani's study. Are we disturbing you at a bad time?"

CHAPTER SEVEN

"I was just finishing up some cleaning before I set the table for dinner," he said. "Please, do come in."

A woman's voice called out from another room. "Nunzio, what's going on?"

Agatha put her index finger to her lips. "*Shhh . . . ,*" she whispered.

"I'm arranging the flowers in the entry hall, Madam Melissa," replied the manservant. "Dinner will be ready in half an hour."

Nunzio led them to the study. As they walked along the hallway, Agatha noted that, like the entrance to the building, it was only lit by small, dim gas lanterns.

"Why is it so cold?" asked Dash, feeling a chill down his spine.

"Mr. Modigliani prefers that the heating be turned down when there are no guests."

"Does he say the same about the lights? This house is really gloomy . . ."

"The master is very thrifty."

Agatha weighed the servant's last words. "That explains why he hasn't had a blacksmith fix the front gate," she said, her eyes gleaming.

"Actually, Miss, I'll be attending to that as soon as I can borrow a welding torch."

"You take care of that sort of thing?"

"I take care of all sorts of repairs, in addition to my other tasks. I'm happy to be of service. The master is always so worried about everything. The restorations, and now the missing crown . . ."

"Did you say restorations?" Chandler interrupted. "What do you mean?"

"Well, it's not really a secret, but Mr. Modigliani prefers not to speak of it," Nunzio said. "The preservation trust is pressuring him to repair this historic building from the ground up, and Mr. Modigliani is trying everything he can to satisfy their requests."

"I imagine that would be very expensive,"

said Agatha, sitting at the mahogany desk in the study.

"I'm afraid so, Miss."

Dash whispered in Agatha's ear. "It's all so clear now! Modigliani needs money to restore the building, and he'll get it from the insurance company. I knew it would be a simple solution!"

Agatha rubbed her hands together to warm them. "Can you please tell us what happened last night?" she asked, turning back to the servant.

"I don't have anything to add to what Mr. Modigliani told you this afternoon. Everything was just as he said."

"And you were in the dining room with him and his guests the whole time?"

"Well, no," he replied, squinting as he tried to recall every detail. "I had to go to the kitchen from time to time to serve the food."

"So you could have come in here to steal the crown," Dash pressed him.

Nunzio looked shocked. "I swear on my honor that I would never have done such a thing!"

The three investigators exchanged glances.

"Very well, then," said Agatha with a big smile. "Now, if you'd like to go and prepare dinner, we'd appreciate being left here for a few minutes to consult."

"Of course, Miss."

As soon as he left, Agatha jumped to her feet and started looking around. "I'm sure that the key to solving this mystery is right in this room."

"It had to be Modigliani," repeated Dash. "But maybe we should add Nunzio to our list of suspects . . ."

Chandler picked Watson up and gave a small cough, as though his own pride were wounded. "If I may, a loyal servant valued by his employer would never commit such an offense," he said. "It goes against all professional ethics."

"You're quite right," observed Agatha

pensively. "And Dash, you're forgetting one little detail," she added.

"What detail?"

"Why wasn't the baron able to find the study when he went to look for his cigars?"

Dash leaned against the cold fireplace, massaging his forehead. "I'm starting to get a headache," he complained. "Obviously the baron just had the wrong room!"

"Are you sure?" Agatha smiled. "All right, let's try to add up the facts. Baron von Horvath insists that he saw an old suit of armor as soon as he opened the door. Yet from the doorway, the fireplace is the first thing you see."

Agatha stood in the doorway, stroking the tip of her nose. She took a few steps forward, then turned and moved toward the armor, crossing the room diagonally. Then she turned around, staring back at the bookcase and mirror. She went back and forth a few more times.

Dash followed her, trying to figure out what she was doing. Then he stopped in front of the tall mirror to crack a joke. "This mirror saw the whole thing: who came in, who left, who opened the window. Too bad it can't talk!"

Agatha stopped in her tracks. "Dash, you're a genius!"

"I am? What brilliant thing did I do?"

"You just solved the case!"

"I did?"

"Yes, you did!" said Agatha, smiling. She explained her theory to Dash and Chandler, who listened intently. Then they all rushed down to the dining room.

Alfredo Modigliani was already seated at the head of the table, reading a newspaper by the weak lamplight. When he heard them enter, he looked up from the metro section and stared at them in amazement. "Where did you come from?" he exclaimed. "Does this mean you have

found the crown, detectives?"

"Yes, sir," Agatha stated. "We know exactly what happened and where it's hidden."

Modigliani's jaw dropped.

"But first, we'd like to ask you a favor."

He dropped the paper and jumped to his feet. "I'm at your disposal," he said. "But who is the thief? You're not going to make me wait?"

"Do as I ask and you'll get a surprise," replied Agatha, smiling.

He listened attentively to Agatha's requests. A moment later he reached for the phone. "All right," he agreed. "I'll make the calls right away."

CHAPTER EIGHT

The Hidden Crown

Nunzio had arranged sofas and chairs for everyone in the front parlor. Their expressions ranged from curious to hostile. Baron von Horvath was squirming in his seat because he had been invited to an auction of archaeological finds that evening. Lord Edwards was taking a break from a poker game and couldn't wait to get back to it. Gonzago and his secret half sister seemed calmer, but everyone looked at one another with guarded suspicion.

"Well?" asked Mr. Modigliani. "We're all here. Let's get started, Miss."

Agatha pulled out her trusty notebook. "The

complexity of this case lies in the fact that any one of you could have committed the crime. After dinner, each of you had the opportunity to make off with the crown." She paused to observe the suspects' reactions, then continued. "The baron could have done it when he went to get his cigars—"

"I protest!" shouted the Hungarian, jumping up from the sofa. "I . . . I . . ."

Agatha raised her voice. "I didn't say it was you. Let me finish, please!"

Von Horvath sat back down grumpily.

"Lord Edwards could have entered the study when he went out to make his private phone call—"

"My dear child, I am no thief!" the English nobleman reacted with anger.

A threatening glance from Chandler quickly silenced him.

"Señor Suárez could have stolen the crown when he left early—"

CHAPTER EIGHT

"But I accompanied him to the door!" protested Mrs. Modigliani.

"You could have been in it together," explained Agatha. "Even Mr. Modigliani could have hidden the crown when he went to fetch the baron's cigars. He went into the study alone, and he was the first to report the theft."

"What are you getting at, Miss?" asked Alfredo Modigliani, stunned. "I'm the one who got robbed! How could I be a suspect?"

"It's even possible," Agatha went on, "that Nunzio could have been the thief. During dinner, he was the only one to go in and out of the dining room."

A heavy cloak of silence fell over the group.

"Any one of you could have stolen the crown," concluded the girl.

"What about the open window?" asked Mr. Modigliani. "Isn't that how the thief got inside?"

"No cat burglar climbed up your wall, sir,"

Agatha said with a smile. "The open window and ivy leaves on the floor were staged by the real culprit."

Modigliani looked offended. "So you're insinuating that it was one of us?"

"I'm not insinuating anything. I'm certain of it."

"But that's impossible!" Gonzago interjected. "We're all gentlemen here."

Agatha gazed at her cousin. "One of our illustrious predecessors once said that after the impossible is eliminated, all that remains is the truth. Isn't that right, Dash?"

Dash had no idea what she was referring to, but he nodded in solemn agreement.

"Go on, Miss," Mr. Modigliani encouraged.

"The impossibility, in this case, was seeing the suit of armor at the entrance to the study," she continued. "But Baron von Horvath was not mistaken, he was simply misled."

CHAPTER EIGHT

"How is that possible?" asked the baron, curious.

"The mirror in the study, at the precise moment you opened the door, had been moved from its usual position," revealed Agatha.

"Explain yourself, Miss!" exclaimed Lord Edwards, stroking his mustache.

"Chandler, if you please," said the girl.

"Follow me," said the butler, leading them all to the study. When they were all inside the room, he moved in front of the mirror and fumbled with the edges. In the silence, they all heard a loud *CLICK*. Chandler slowly moved the mirror on two hinges.

"As you can see," Agatha continued, "the mirror opens toward the entrance to the room. When it is completely open, all that can be seen from the threshold is a reflection of the suit of armor to the right of the door."

Everyone stood in stunned silence.

"Mr. Modigliani, who knew that the mirror could be moved?" asked Agatha.

"I have to admit that I knew," he replied. "There is a compartment behind the mirror where I keep important family documents."

"So, Modigliani, you're responsible for the theft!" cried the Spaniard.

"Mr. Modigliani couldn't have stolen the crown," Agatha continued confidently. "He was in the dining room with the baron when the theft took place. The thief entered the study, took the crown from the desk, opened the mirror, and hid it inside that secret compartment. At that very moment, the baron arrived at the door, but he didn't see anyone in the room—the mirror goes all the way to the floor, hiding the culprit's feet. After von Horvath withdrew, the thief quickly replaced the mirror, then opened the window and scattered some ivy leaves to make it look like that was how they came in."

CHAPTER EIGHT

Agatha looked each of them in the eyes. "But that plan was foiled," she added, "because someone else found the crown and took it from its hiding place!"

"No!" shouted Mrs. Modigliani, as white as a ghost. "No! That was my future! My only hope for a new life!" She launched herself at the compartment behind the mirror, searching frantically. "I left it right there! It was here! It's mine! Mine!"

Gonzago looked upset. "Melissa, what did you do?" he whispered.

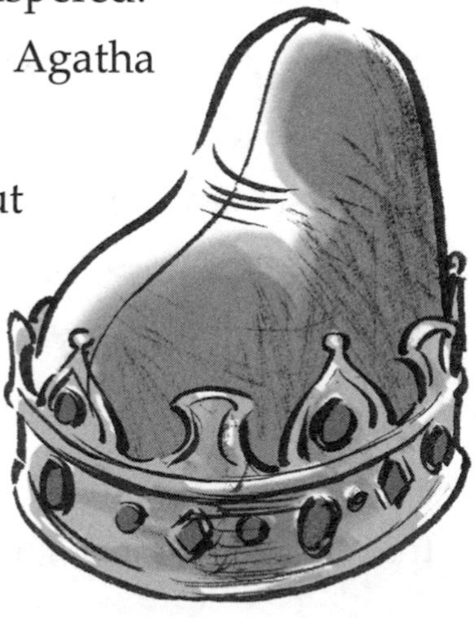

Turning to Chandler, Agatha asked for the crown.

The butler pulled it out from under his jacket and held it up for all to see.

"Don't worry, Mrs. Modigliani, it's perfectly

safe," said Agatha calmly. "The butler did it. We just needed to hear you confess."

Melissa collapsed onto a chair, overcome with tears.

"Perhaps you could tell us the whole story," Agatha encouraged her gently.

Through her sobs, Melissa began to speak. "I was so tired of the life I've been living, and when I found out that Gonzago was my half brother, I realized I had a chance to escape, to change everything—"

"My dear," interrupted Modigliani. "What are you talking about?"

"Everything! I've had enough! Ever since we got married, you've kept me stuck in this gloomy museum. All you care about is your good name and your famous family. Every penny we have gets spent on this cursed house. If you had been willing to sell the crown, we could have restored the building and still had enough left over to live a good life. But not you! You'd rather hold on to your past and sit here in the dark, like a fossil! I just wanted to be happy!"

After this outburst, Melissa Modigliani lowered her voice. "That's why I stole the crown. I would have sold it and moved to Spain. After I saw Gonzago to the door, I went up to my room and just stared at the ceiling. Then it occurred to me that the crown was still sitting right there on your desk. I knew about your secret compartment behind the mirror, of course," she said with a sad little smile. "I know every inch of this dreary old house. And if the baron hadn't come looking for his cigars, and that nosy girl hadn't come along . . . I'd be on my way to sunny Spain, happy and free!"

Melissa started to cry again. Gonzago tried awkwardly to console her as her husband stared at them both in shock.

Lord Edwards and Baron von Horvath exchanged glances and rose to their feet.

"Dear Modigliani, call if you need us," they said, almost in unison. Nodding a hasty good-bye, they left the palazzo in silence.

While Gonzago did his best to calm Melissa, Dash and Agatha turned to her husband.

"What do you plan to do now?" asked Agatha.

Modigliani shook his head heavily. "I think I have been a very bad husband," he whispered guiltily. "I knew that my wife wasn't happy, but I could never have imagined this . . ." He raised his eyes to meet hers. "Thank you, each and all. This has made me realize many mistakes I've made. Please don't turn in my wife. I love her, and I'll do my best to repair all the damage I've caused. Could you please inform the insurance company?"

"Of course," said Dash. "We'll tell them it was a simple misunderstanding."

"After all," Agatha reassured him, "the doge's crown was right here all along."

CHAPTER EIGHT

They left the palazzo in silence and stopped on the dock to gaze out at the beautiful city. Venice looked like a dream, with the moon reflected in the rippling canal. Chandler suggested they call Marco's cell phone to let him know about their success.

When the gondolier arrived, they all climbed on board.

"Take us wherever you like, dear cousin," exclaimed Agatha. "We have a great story to tell you!"

Marco nodded, pushing away from the red-and-white striped pole at the dock. As the gondola slid over the shimmering water, he threw back his head and began to sing. Watson, curled up on Chandler's lap, joined in with his own loud yowls.

Dash and Agatha laughed loud and long; they had completed yet another challenging mission!

EPILOGUE

Mystery Solved . . .

They all spent the night at the Bucintoro, a charming small hotel in the Arsenal district. Marco knew the owner, and recommended it for its excellent hospitality.

Before they went to bed, Agatha dragged Dash into a cozy parlor lit with soft lights. The walls were covered with pictures of all sizes. "Notice anything, cousin?" she asked, fixing her eyes on the portraits.

"I'm half asleep," Dash grumbled. "Who are all these weirdos?"

Agatha rubbed her nose. "I'll give you a hint: They're all wearing peaked purple crowns."

"Some kind of traditional Carnevale hat?" guessed the bumbling detective.

"Dash! They're portraits of the doges!"

Dash fell silent as he gazed at each face. Agatha whispered, "If my memory serves me correctly, the Hotel Bucintoro is named after the luxurious boat that the doges used to travel the Grand Canal."

"That must be it!" said Dash, pointing to a large painting in the center. It showed an ornately carved ship with at least twenty oars on each side. "Talk about bling! It looks like it's made of pure gold!"

"We couldn't have ended up at a more perfect hotel after today's adventure!" Agatha said with a wink. "Sweet dreams, cousin!"

The next morning, the sun shone so brightly that the canals looked like turquoise. Before flying home, they decided to bask in the city's magical atmosphere just a bit longer. Chandler called Marco and arranged to meet him for lunch on the Rialto.

Dash was filled with confidence after receiving a congratulatory message from Eye International. Without pausing to look at a map, he launched himself into the winding Venetian alleys. "We deserve a vacation!" he kept saying at every corner. "Who can beat us? Nobody! We're the best detectives in the world!"

The others let him gloat as they made their way through the festive crowd, stopping to look at historical landmarks that Agatha wanted to see. After the third art-filled church, she put down her guidebook and pointed to a shop selling Carnevale costumes. "I think it's time we joined the party!" she exclaimed with a gleam in her eye.

"I agree, Miss," replied the square-jawed Chandler.

Her cousin looked around blankly. "Party? What party?"

Agatha and Chandler had already stepped into the shop and were looking for costumes in their sizes. They each tried on several, laughing when Watson meowed at a black mask. Agatha fixed the elastic to fit behind his ears. "Look!" she exclaimed. "He's a cat burglar!"

EPILOGUE

They went back to Piazza San Marco to meet their gondolier cousin. He arrived right on time, singing at the top of his lungs as he tied up his boat and scanned the busy square, ignoring the small group of masked revelers who stood on the dock right in front of him. "They must be lost," he muttered. "Englishmen always get lost."

Just then, an enormous hairy gorilla approached.

"Sorry, I'm on a break," the gondolier said politely.

A lanky boy dressed as Batman joined the gorilla.

"This gondola is unavailable right now, I'm afraid!"

Finally, a young girl in a Sherlock Holmes outfit stepped forward.

"I'm waiting for some friends—"

It wasn't until cat-burglar Watson jumped into the gondola and began rubbing against Marco's legs that he finally realized who these strange people were. He started to laugh. "You got me!" he cried with a giant grin. "You're unrecognizable! Now, what do you say we go have some lunch in a fabulous Venetian restaurant? I'll be the one in the gondolier costume!"

They all agreed enthusiastically. As they strolled across the square, they filled Marco in on their investigation. Marco was thrilled with his English cousins' adventures.

"Just business as usual," Dash said with a shrug. "If I were to tell you how many cases we've solved . . ."

He heard a loud *BLIP* and pulled his EyeNet out of his pocket. "Another congratulatory message," he sighed. But no, it was his friends Clarke and Mallory, begging him to continue their game of *Alien Hunt*. Dash's EyeNet was always connected to his home computer in London, and he was about to join his friends in the game when he felt a tug on his cape. He turned around and was astonished to see the girl in the Cinderella costume.

"Umm . . . still very busy . . . making that film for my school report . . . ," he muttered.

"Yeah, right!" she said with a smirk.

"Uh, what do you mean?"

The beautiful Cinderella crossed her arms over her chest. "That titanium gadget isn't a video camera," she said. "It's something else!"

"Wh-what?" said Dash, noticing that his companions were laughing together.

"It's a gaming console!" said Cinderella. "And you just logged on to my favorite game, *Alien Hunt*!"

Dash's eyes lit up. "You know *Alien Hunt*?"

"Know it? I rule it!"

"Oh yeah? What's your code name?"

She twirled around, so her blue skirt flared like a bell. "Isn't it obvious? I'm Killderella!"

Dash turned white.

He had faced an opponent named Killderella many times, and lost every single game. Killderella was the game's top slayer, ranked first in the world.

"No way!" he exclaimed. "I'm Phil Destroy!"

She doubled over in laughter. "Ha-ha! You're roadkill, Phil Destroy! I've annihilated you at least a dozen times!"

"Uh, well, that's true." Dash was very embarrassed, but he was also thrilled. He scratched his chin and asked awkwardly, "Umm . . . could you teach me some of your moves? I'm just about to play a game now . . ."

The beautiful Cinderella, also known by her battle name Killderella, flashed a smug grin. "See you online sometime soon, Phil Destroy," she whispered in a challenging tone. "Like I said yesterday, not cool to leave a nice girl like me by herself!"

Dash watched her strut away, biting his tongue as he rejoined his friends. "You're a real idiot, Dash Mistery." He sighed. "All that physiognomy you studied is useless if you don't recognize the girl of your dreams when you meet her!"

Agatha

Girl of Mystery

Agatha's Next Mystery:

The Kenyan Expedition

PRELUDE

The Investigation Begins . . .

In a central-London penthouse packed full of high-tech devices lived young Dashiell Mistery, an aspiring detective with a passion for technology. He was not an organized person, and pieces in his collection often met with unfortunate ends: an MP3 player frozen in the freezer, a laptop drowned in the bathtub, a video-game controller liquefied in the microwave . . .

Only one object was worthy of Dash's full attention: his EyeNet, a valuable tool that Eye International Detective Academy—Dash's school—provided for its students. The EyeNet was a mass of futuristic features encased in a titanium shell, and the young Londoner kept it hanging above the sofa so that it was never out of his sight.

One Saturday afternoon in late April, Dash was busy tinkering with an old radio with bent antennae. The floor was already a chaotic mess of electronic components, wires, transistors, and other materials recovered from unused appliances. While carefully removing the internal circuits and putting them on the carpet, he continually flicked his gaze at the device to check that it was in its place. It was two o'clock. Dash put the old radio aside to hurriedly scarf down a sandwich before moving on to his next project.

The previous week, he had taken a videoconference course in Subterfuge and Escapes, a discipline detailing techniques for getting oneself off the hook using only talent and whatever tools were at hand. The instructor for the course, codename GC43, was nicknamed MacGyver in honor of the famous television series.

Dash had subsequently thrown himself headlong into the study of electronics and a frenzy of new projects. With the radio dismantled, Dash's main task for today was to record the notes from his electric guitar directly onto his computer using wiring of his own invention. He completed the final steps and hoisted up his gleaming red guitar by the neck, adopting a rock-star pose.

He inserted the plug into the computer. Squinting at his monitor to check the frequencies, he positioned his hands on the strings and launched into a Led Zeppelin solo.

SBRANGGGGGG!!!

The speakers let out a noise so loud that it made the glass in his fifteenth-floor windows vibrate. The shock wave threw the slender boy across the room, and a stunned expression covered his face. "I for-forgot to unplug the st-stereo system!" he exclaimed to himself.

As if that weren't enough, a piercing alarm suddenly sounded, followed by a panicked shout. He had frightened the other inhabitants of Baker Place nearly to death!

"I have to do something!" he cried, pushing a mess of electronics under the table. "If they figure out it was me, I'm done for!"

He covered the jumbled pile with a sheet, barely a moment before there was a knock at the door.

"Dash Mistery!" someone called. "It was you—that noise came from in there!"

"Get out here and face the music!" someone added.

Judging from the angry voices, it seemed that a line of protestors had filled the hallway.

Dash ran his hands through his disheveled hair and approached the door with cautious steps. "Who is it?" he asked innocently.

A chorus of complaints sounded from outside. Dash released the security chain and peered out just enough to see at least twenty people crowded near his door. He gulped. "Did you feel that terrible earthquake, too?" he asked. "It's all over the news . . ."

"Don't mess around with us!" shouted the landlord of the building, a gray-haired lawyer wearing a suit of the same color. "You're in enough trouble as it is!" He waved a piece of paper under Dash's nose. It could only be an eviction notice. "This is the last straw, Mr. Mistery," he added sternly.

Dash's legs turned to jelly. "But, I–I—" he stammered. "I didn't do anything!"

"The electric guitar!" interrupted the neighbor from the apartment directly below, a woman with a shrill voice who worked in finance. "I heard that demonic instrument just before the alarm went off!"

"I wasn't playing a guitar. I don't even own one, trust me!"

More complaints erupted. "He's telling lies! The regulations prohibit musical instruments! Evict him!" shouted a chorus of the elegant building's tenants.

"We need proof," the landlord interrupted, trying to calm tempers. "Let me in, Mr. Mistery. I would like to see for myself that you don't have a guitar."

"Um . . . of course . . . come in."

The man entered and inspected the room with hawklike eyes. "Where is it hidden?" he growled. "Under the sheet?"

The young detective shrugged. "Take a look, if you like. It's just a bunch of circuits and other equipment. I work with advanced electronics," he said with indifference, reclining on the sofa. The soft cushions hid the shape of the guitar.

The search continued for several long minutes, but in the end the landlord had to give up. "Very well, Mr. Mistery," he declared in disappointment. "Without the offending item, I can't evict you."

"What did I tell you?" Dash grinned, gesturing toward the door from his spot on the couch. Just then, the EyeNet began flashing furiously. It was his school signaling that he had a new mission!

Dash grabbed the EyeNet, threw on a jacket, and slipped out past the other tenants who were still grumbling on the crowded landing. He pulled the door tightly closed behind him and ran for the elevator.

As he reached the elevator, the he checked the EyeNet screen. "An investigation in Kenya?" he shrieked.

Fortunately for him, he knew exactly where to find his cousin and incomparable companion in adventure, Agatha Mistery.

Withdrawn